Colin Thiele

FARMER SCHULZ'S DUCKS

ILLUSTRATED BY

Mary Milton

HARPER & ROW, PUBLISHERS

Farmer Schulz's Ducks

Text copyright © 1986 by Colin Thiele
Illustrations copyright © 1986 by Mary Milton
First published in Australia by Walter McVitty Books, Glebe, N.S.W.
All rights reserved. No part of this book may be
used or reproduced in any manner whatsoever without
written permission except in the case of brief
quotations embodied in critical articles and reviews.
Printed in the United States of America.
For information address Harper & Row Junior Books,
10 East 53rd Street, New York, N.Y. 10022.
Typography by Andrew Rhodes
      3   4   5   6   7   8   9   10

Library of Congress Cataloging-in-Publication Data

Thiele, Colin.
Farmer Schulz's ducks / Colin Thiele:
illustrated by Mary Milton.—1st American ed.
   p.   cm.
   Summary: After the growing traffic from the nearby city turns
the road next to their Australian farm into a dangerous highway,
Farmer Schulz's youngest daughter Anna solves the problem of how to
get her family's ducks safely across the road every day.
   ISBN 0-06-026182-X : $
   ISBN 0-06-026183-8 (lib. bdg.) : $
   [1. Ducks—Fiction. 2. Australia—Fiction] I. Milton, Mary, ill.
II. Title. PZ7.T354Far 1988   87-21713
[E]—dc19   CIP
                                       AC

Farmer Schulz's Ducks

In the hills of South Australia there is a little river with a big name—the Onkaparinga. It flowed through a valley full of apple trees and cabbage patches, pastures and gardens, red gum trees and poplars.

In springtime blossoms fell like confetti, as if the hills were having a wedding, and there was celery on the breath of the wind.

In autumn the willows bowed down by the river, their branches like arches of gold.

And in winter the tall trees whipped the air in the wind and the rain, and the high water in the river went fussing and gurgling on its crooked way.

A narrow road wound down the valley. Sometimes it ran by the side of the river and sometimes it veered away. And it ran right past the front gate of Farmer Schulz's farm, between his house and the Onkaparinga River.

Farmer Schulz was a busy man, and his farm was a busy place. There were cows in the paddocks. There were geese on the pastures and goats on the hillsides. There were pear trees and apple, carrots and cucumbers, berries and bacon. There were furrows combed out for potatoes, and trellises like wigwams for beans.

The beams of the cellar were loaded with German sausage, and the shelves held dishes of scalded cream.

And in the yard at the back of the house there were more than fifty ducks.

Farmer Schulz's ducks were the most beautiful in the world. There were brown ducks and gray ducks and speckled ducks. There were ducks with necks of opal and wings of amethyst; their colors gleamed in the sunlight, their feathers shone like jewels. There were ducks with the sheen of emerald, of sapphire and turquoise and jasper, like the glint of Aladdin's treasure. There were ducks like burnished gold.

There were drakes as well—brown drakes, mottled drakes, muddy drakes. Drakes with eyes like night and bills like scoops. There were great white drakes with noses redder than roses. And ducklings as tiny as tennis balls and as soft as clusters of golden wattle when it bloomed on the hills by the Onkaparinga River.

Every morning after breakfast Farmer Schulz opened the backyard gate so that the ducks could go down to the river. They took their time, even when they were in a hurry to reach the water. They held their heads high and waddled with dignity, even though they had to jostle each other when they went through the gate. The ducklings hurried to line up behind their mothers.

They went quickly down the drive by the side of the house and poured out across the road on their way to the Onkaparinga River. Sometimes a car would go by, or a trailer loaded high with meadow hay, or a tractor coughing in the frosty morning air. The drivers always stopped, because everyone knew that the ducks had the right of way.

All day long the ducks swam in the pools of the peaceful and weedy river. They explored the reeds and tugged at the waterweeds and dug at the muddy banks. They floated like petals and sailed like boats with their webbed feet paddling hard. They waddled onto shore and blinked their eyes and used their bills like spades.

But at sunset they all went home.

For when the shadows deepened and the valley was blue with haze, there were nasty things by the side of the Onkaparinga River. There were wild cats with eyes like ice and claws like steel; there were slinking foxes as crafty as serpents and as silent as falling dew; and there were hunters with shotguns. So the drakes led the way back home, and the ducks and the ducklings hurried along in a line.

Farmer Schulz was proud of their wisdom. "Good boys," he said to the drakes. "Good girls, good little children," he said to the ducks and ducklings. "Now safe from the fox you will be. Now we all in peace can sleep."

As the years went by the number of people grew. The city beyond the hills became as fat as a big balloon. More houses were built in the valley by the side of the gentle river, and lines of cars like strings of beads went racing down the road. They raced away in the morning and they all raced back in the evening. The drivers were always late. They blew their horns, and shouted loudly and rudely, and accelerated much too quickly.

Sometimes they didn't even stop for the ducks!

One Christmas Eve a drake was run over and had to be added to the Christmas dinner.

Farmer Schulz was red with rage. "We must this nonsense stop!" he cried. "We must put up a big notice for the ducks." And he called his family together to think of the right words.

DUCKS COMMING HERE he wrote. But Farmer Schulz's son Hans laughed and said it wasn't even English.

"Crossing ducks," suggested Gretchen. Some liked that, but others did not.

"Ducks cross here," ventured Adolf, but his mother said that people would think it was a place for angry ducks.

"Stop for ducks," suggested Helga, but Hans said it would make everyone think there were ducks for sale.

Four-year-old Anna, who was rolling breadcrumbs into a ball, looked up suddenly. "Why don't you say 'ducks crossing'?" she asked. "Because that's what they're always doing."

"Wonderful!" said her father. "You are smarter than Einstein, Anna."

"Great!" said Gretchen.

"Brilliant!" said Hans.

And so Anna's sign was painted and nailed to a post by the side of the road.

The sign was not a success. Some cars stopped, but others did not. This made the crossing more dangerous than ever. And then one morning there was a terrible accident.

A truck slowed down when the ducks were coming from Farmer Schulz's drive. But not the driver who came racing along behind it. He swerved out of his lane without even seeing if the way was clear. He accelerated to pass the truck. He drove headlong into the waddling ducks. *Crash!*

There were shouts and cries and squealing tires. There were gabbles and quacks and flying feathers. Four ducks had concussions and had to be nursed in a box beside the kitchen fire. Two drakes had broken legs and had to wear splints for months. And three little ducklings were dead. Anna buried them beside the lettuce.

Farmer Schulz's face was the color of one of his favorite ducks—mottled and blue and purple with anger. "Lunatic!" he shouted. "Silly ass!"

"Give up," said Hans. "Sell the ducks before all of them are killed."

"Never!" answered Farmer Schulz furiously. "Never, never."

"Then build a house on the other side of the road. Build a house by the river."

"Never. Why for should I move my house when it is not my fault?"

"Then we'd better teach them to fly," said Anna. "They can't cross the road anymore unless they go over the top."

Farmer Schulz opened his eyes wide. "Over the top? Of course!" He slapped his hand on his thigh.

"You are smarter than Einstein, Anna. From now on the ducks will go over the top."

Hans was flabbergasted. "How are you going to manage that?" he asked.

His father's mind was running at a feverish pitch. "With a bridge, of course. Then the people can drive like lunatics if they want. My ducks will be safe. They will go over the top."

He brought two tall poles and put them up beside his drive about three feet apart. Then he put another two by the fence on the river side. And between them he slung the trunks of two long pine trees, like beams, more than twelve feet above the road—an overpass with safety fences of wire mesh at the sides, and two long ramps at the ends for the ducks to walk up and down.

Before long the ducks knew the way. When they came out of their yard they went straight to the ramp. Then, with waddling feet and quacking, they hurried up—and across—and down. It was a wonderful sight: a procession of ducks against the sky.

Before long the cars were all stopping to watch them. Even the drivers who had no time for the ducks on the ground now stopped to watch them pass overhead.

Soon the Bridge of Ducks was famous. People came in carloads. They came with cameras, and they posed for pictures with a line of ducks behind them. They trampled the grass like buffaloes. Poor Farmer Schulz was beside himself!

Then disaster struck on the first of March. The ducks were coming out of the Onkaparinga River and waddling toward the ramp. Farmer Schulz had just stopped his tractor and was stretching his weary arms. At that very moment a monstrous semitrailer came roaring around the bends of the narrow road. The driver was new to the valley, and he was late with his goods for the city. He was driving too fast. He was tired and sleepy.

And his load was too high for the bridge!

The ducks were waddling across the overpass, hurrying and quacking as they went.

The semitrailer came roaring around the corner like a cyclone. It struck the bridge at the center, shattering the beams like matchsticks. The ducks were flung like flotsam—backward, forward, upward, sideways—trumpeting and shrieking. Some landed back in the river. Some flew, some fell, some leaped. Some were hurled along the side of the road, some even into their own backyard. Some were unharmed. Some were hurt. And some were dead.

It took a long time for Farmer Schulz to recover from the shock. He had to clear away the wreckage of the bridge. He had to breed more ducks. And he was in trouble with the government for building an overpass without permission. "You can't build bridges wherever you like," the government said. "There could have been a terrible accident."

"There *was* a terrible accident," Farmer Schulz said angrily.

Once more there was a family meeting.

"Give up," said Hans. "Get rid of the ducks while you can."

"Never!" answered his father. "The ducks are part of the family. They are like brothers and sisters, nearly."

"But how in the world are they going to cross the road? They have to go down to the water."

"We must all think," his father said. "We must all think hard."

"There's no point in building another bridge," Hans said. "It will simply be smashed again."

Little Anna had come home from kindergarten and was busy rolling breadcrumbs, as usual. "Why don't you have a pipe," she said, "so the ducks can cross under the road?"

There was silence for a while, and then the others raised their eyebrows in amazement.

"Wonderful!" exclaimed her mother.

"Brilliant!" cried Hans.

"By golly, Anna, you are smarter than Einstein, even!" shouted her father, with eyes as wide as an owl's.

This time Farmer Schulz was going to do it right. He wrote an official letter to the government. He drew up a plan for everyone to see. He went from one building to another building, from one floor to another floor, from one person to another person. He had to fill in one form and another form, and wait in one room and another room. It was almost more than Farmer Schulz could bear—just to put a duck pipe underneath the road. For nobody had ever heard of such a thing before.

There were water pipes and sewer pipes and drain pipes and fuel pipes; there were cable pipes and steam pipes and oil pipes and gas pipes. There were copper pipes and steel pipes, plastic pipes and concrete pipes, and a hundred other pipes besides. But nowhere had there ever been a duck pipe before.

"A duck pipe?" They laughed. "You must be joking."

Farmer Schulz was red with anger and blue with impatience and purple with frustration. "It is no joke," he roared. "My ducks are never joking."

But the government told him to go home quietly and wait.

Farmer Schulz waited. He milked his cows and planted potatoes and picked apples—and he bred more ducks. And at last, after waiting for twelve months and twenty-three days, Farmer Schulz was allowed to build his pipe. It was a beautiful pipe, three feet in diameter and one hundred and

eighty feet long. It went under the ground at the side of the house and it came out near the bank of the gently flowing Onkaparinga River.

Farmer Schulz built flaps of wire mesh at each end to guide the ducks in. They hustled and quacked at first, trying to learn the way. Farmer Schulz shooed and Mrs. Schulz shushed. Hans and Gretchen and Helga and Adolf held out their arms and flapped. And little Anna clapped her hands when at last the ducks went through. Everyone kissed her and said she was smarter than Einstein to think of a plan like that.

After that there was peace at last. All day long the ducks lazed by the riverside, listening to the secrets of the earth and the words of the running water. They could hear the grass growing and the small seeds stretching and the earthworms moving under the ground. They snoozed in the sunshine with their heads tucked under, or floated on the river as softly as blossoms.

Shortly afterward one of Farmer Schulz's friends carved a life-sized duck from a piece of marble and placed it on a pillar of stone by the side of the road. Then he carved two words in the stone for all to see: DUCK DORF, the village of ducks. Farmer Schulz looked at it and grinned. He was as happy and contented as he had ever been.

That year Farmer Schulz won three blue ribbons at the Show, and a Grand Champion Medal for a flinty-eyed drake. He was as proud as a peacock and as boastful as a fisherman.

"My ducks," he said loudly, "are the best and the smartest in the whole wide world."

The ducks were contented too. It was wonderful to see them streaming out of the pipe in the morning, like ants coming out of the ground, and to watch them hurrying back in the evening, like beetles bound for their burrows.

In the summer the pipe gave them shelter from the heat. In winter, when the rain poured down and the water swept out of the pipe in a torrent, they came skidding and skiing, swimming and splashing, in a wild, rollicking rush—a waterfall of ducks. In the spring they came out into a magic land that was white with blossom, and in autumn they waddled out onto a carpet of golden leaves.

They are still there now, dawdling and dabbling happily where the willows arch and sway by the banks of the beautiful Onkaparinga River.